Cat in the Manger

A Red Fox Book

Published by Random House Children's Books
20 Vauxhall Bridge Road, London SW1V 2SA

Copyright © Michael Foreman 2000

1 3 5 7 9 10 8 6 4 2

First published in Great Britain by Andersen Press Ltd 2000
Red Fox edition 2001

The right of Michael Foreman to be identified as the author and illustrator of this work
has been asserted by him in accordance with the Copyright, Designs and Patents Act, 1988.

Printed in Hong Kong by Midas Printing Ltd

THE RANDOM HOUSE GROUP Limited Reg. No. 954009

www.randomhouse.co.uk

ISBN 0 09 940755 8

Cat in the Manger

MICHAEL FOREMAN

RED FOX

Now, I've got nothing against cows. They may be a bit stupid and clumsy, bumping into each other as they do, but at least they are warm. On a cold night they heat the old barn up a treat. And, if I sleep in the manger, I don't get trodden on.

It was really cold that night, I remember. A dusting of snow, and bright, bright stars, so I was glad the old cows were there to keep me warm.

I don't like goats much. Always arguing and butting each other. Fidgets, the lot of them. It's difficult to get to sleep when there are goats around.

Of course, I'm not meant to sleep. I'm supposed to be catching mice.

Don't talk to me about donkeys. I can't stand donkeys. They look at you with those big eyes as if they're friendly, then they turn around and kick you. You have to watch out when there are donkeys around.

Fortunately, we don't normally have to put up with donkeys in our barn. But this night, just as the barn was getting nice and warm, the door flew open and there was a man and a woman in a flurry of snowflakes with, you've guessed it, a donkey.

The donkey did the usual donkey thing, looking all meek and mild and doing his 'big eye' thing, but he wasn't fooling me. I kept out of the way, safe in the manger.

The man pulled some fresh straw down from the loft and made a bed for the woman in the corner furthest from the door. She didn't look too well.

She cried out once or twice but the man hugged her, and the donkey went even more dewy-eyed. I just minded my own business.

Then I heard a baby cry.
That's all we needed. A crying baby!

The cows and the goats were all wide awake now, shuffling about and treading on each other's toes. Then I was tipped out of the manger!

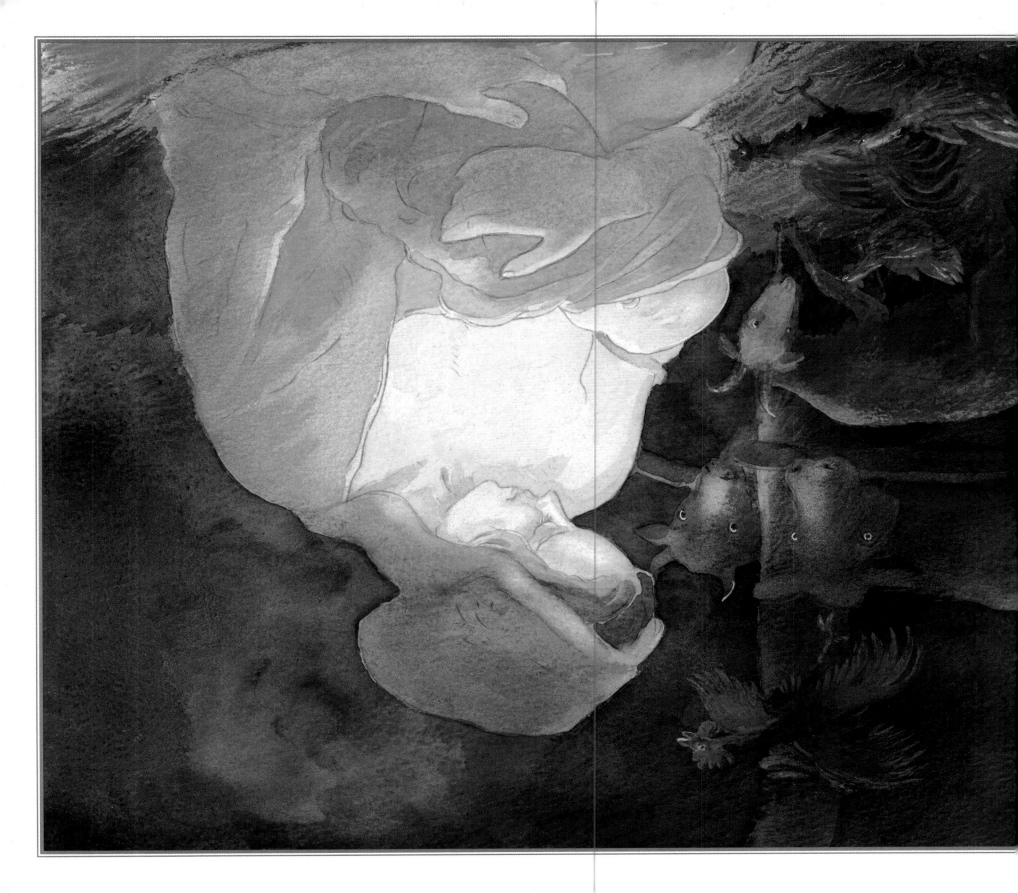

Then all the shuffling stopped.
The baby wasn't crying. Everything
was silent. It was as if all the animals
held their breath. It was as if the
whole world held its breath, and we
all looked at the baby, and the baby
looked at us.

Then I heard sheep. Bleating sheep. Typical! Of all the stupid animals in the world, sheep can be relied upon to be the most stupid. We could hear them coming closer and closer, and then, with an icy blast, the door flew open again and in stumbled some shepherds and snowy sheep.

The shepherds knelt on the mud floor and talked to the man and the woman and smiled at the baby.

The camels were the last straw. They are as clumsy as cows but have much bigger feet, bad tempers, bad breath, and they spit. There were three of them. . .

Enormous they were. They just stuck their heads under the sacks covering the window and glared at us.

I must say their bridles looked smart, red and green leather with gold decorations. And when their three masters strode into the barn, they looked fabulous. They looked as rich as kings.

They knelt with the shepherds, and then all the animals in the barn knelt, as best we could. Even the clumsy cows.

Above, I could see chickens and doves silent in the rafters, and when I looked behind me, I saw rows and rows of mice.

Mice! Behind me! Their beady little eyes flickered from me to the baby and back again.

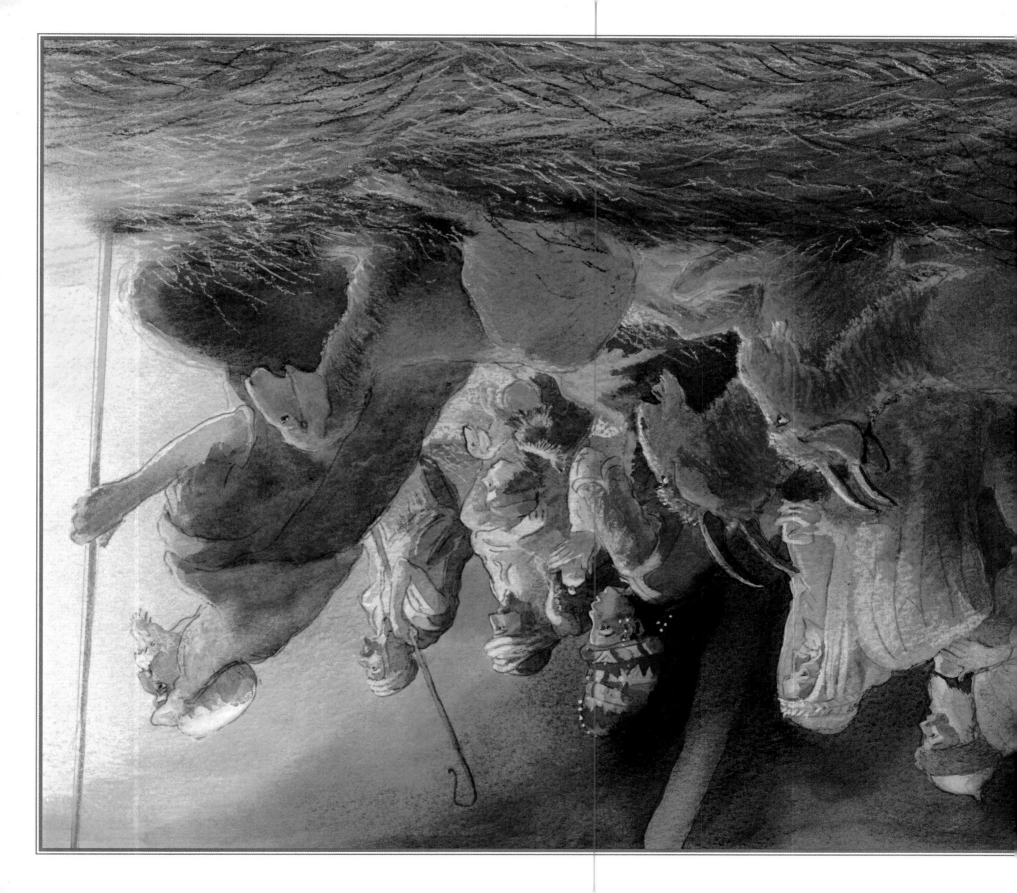

Just this once, I thought, and turned my gaze back to the baby.

The mice crept forward, passed me, and scampered through to the front . . .

*I*t all seems a long time ago now.

Soon everyone had gone.
The shepherds with their bleating
sheep, the rich men with their
grumpy camels, even the man
and the woman with their baby.

I never heard of them again.

Funny thing is, I haven't caught a mouse since. I chase them occasionally, just to keep up appearances . . . But I haven't had the heart to catch one.

More Red Fox picture books
for you to enjoy